I0712780

SAFKINSOP

Dealings with
a Very Dangerous Vampire

By David O'Boyle
Illustrated by Tan Ngo

Paperback ISBN: 979-8-9885674-5-5
EBook ISBN: 979-8-9885674-6-2

For Bram Stoker,
who gave us DRACULA

For Charles Bukowski,
who showed me
a different type of poetry.

When possible,
and in New York City it is always possible,
Vampires feed on
outcasts and vagabonds,
shut-ins, immigrants, and eccentrics,
anyone
they can digest
while maintaining a low profile.

That sort of behavior helps
avoid the police...

...and more specifically,
avoid a referral from
the general police detail,
to a small,
specialized unit
known formally
on the tax records,
as "Police Aid",
yet known informally
as Stokers.
Stokers hunt vampires.
While it's an ancient profession,
it has suffered
from inconsistent naming conventions.
Dracula, published in 1897,
and the subsequent demand
it created for anything vampire
changed all that.
In honor of Dracula's author, Bram Stoker,
we made the title of our vocation more uniform.
Now, everywhere around the globe,
regardless of local language,
we are all stokers.

The title has taken on higher esteem as of late.
This is because killing a vampire is not
as easy as it used to be.

Alongside humans,
the undead have evolved.
In practice, this means that
silver bullets still work,
but it takes an anti-aircraft gun
worth of ammo
to merely stun them.

The same goes for wooden stakes.
You want to kill bloodsuckers that way?
Then you better come ready
to poke them full as a pin cushion,

and do so using
local timber,
a prized commodity in New
York City.

Wood from here is nearly
impossible to find.

Unless, of course,
you want to try
your hand
at lumberjacking
Central Park.

Personally
I'd rather sleep in the coffin
with the vampire I'm trying to kill
then face the wrath
of one of those tree-hugging
urban slackliners
that I'd make fall in the process.

Evolution of the vampire
and the new-age complexities
that come with bringing down the bloodsuckers
has brought increased prestige to our trade.
Barrier to entry is harder than ever.
You can't just be an angry farmer
with a sharpened walking stick
and a dead daughter anymore.
Good news for me, I suppose,
given I get paid to kill them.

And lord have I killed them.
In half a century
I've killed thousands of these bastards.
Pretty much wrote the field guide,
modernizing standard practice.
If you are a stoker
you either know me
or know my name.

Such peer esteem
may be welcome
in a referral-driven business.

All it gets me in the Stoker
unit
of the police
department
are the biggest jobs,
none of which,
was bigger
than the Safkinsop assignment.

Why?
Because the Vampire Safkinsop
had an "estimated conversion amount"
or ECA, of 95%.
This is just our fancy name for one of
the more important vampire metrics.

In plain language,
it means that 95% of the time
Safkinsop delivers a wet bite.
We hate wet bites.
I repeat. We hate wet bites.

Wet bites turn
people into vampires.
To put Safkinsop's ECA
in perspective,
records indicate
that the average vampire
wet bites 20% of the time.
That means
when we are dealing with Safkinsop
we are dealing with a
very
dangerous
vampire.

The relationship between
humans and
dry vampire bites
is a little more
complicated.

It's true that they aren't terminal
but dry bites do
come with their own
set of complications.
You see,
dry bites are delivered
to people that a vampire
finds attractive
during reproductive foreplay.

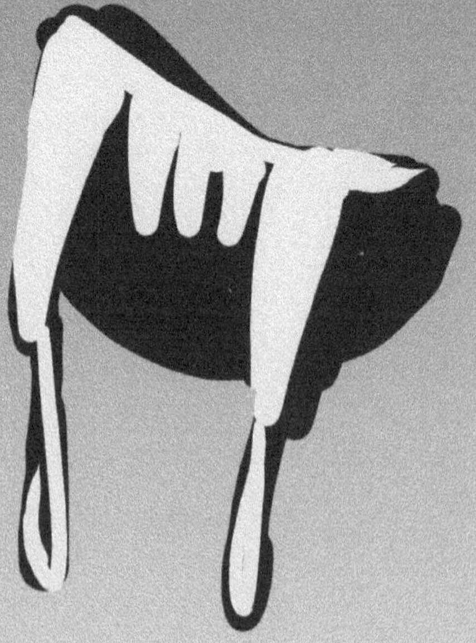

While more research is needed on
the long-term effects of dry bites,
current medical consensus
is that they are innocuous
besides the fact that
if circumstances are right
meaning the female-human
or female-vampire
is of child-rearing age
pregnancy may occur.
Usually such pregnancies arise
from male-vampire and female-human intercourse.
Thankfully, male vampires aren't much interested
in human-women
of child-bearing age.
To them, young people are intolerable,
not to mention delicious.
Taste and intolerance
amounts to a lot of wet bites on the youth.
What also amounts
to a lot of wet bites on the youth
is that Vampires live in fear
of 'natural' reproduction
of getting a human pregnant
of producing...
a manpire.

The problem here is not manpires.
Manpires are living
and can function in society
as well as a human
conceived by two humans.
Leaving their predisposition
for crime aside
a manpire's main problem
is their father.

It's a little sad, actually,
because daddy vampires
intend to be excellent fathers
and would rather be stoked
than abandon their baby manpires.
I say 'intend' to be excellent fathers
rather than 'male vampires are excellent fathers'
because in actuality,
unless a stoker gets to the vampire first
everyone in that manpire's life
that isn't direct bloodline
will be bitten.
Talk about trauma.
This is the basis
for the manpire
nature versus nurture debate
regarding what is responsible
for their often
reprobate
lifestyles
and limited positive contribution
to regular society.
As a general proposition
they don't vote and they don't pay taxes.
And as you will see later
the majority of manpires
tend to make money
amorally.

Female vampires are a little different
when it comes to
their biting predispositions.
While they occasionally seek
human lovers,
vampire women
of child-rearing age
are limited in number.
While they can live hundreds
even thousands of years,
their reproductive window
mirrors that of their
human-female counterparts.

And even if
the female-vampire is
of reproductive age
and gets pregnant,
which can only
happen from a
male-human,
the chances of infanticide
are high
on account of
male-vampire jealousy.

Thus, even female-vampires
who deliver dry bites during
sexual foreplay with a male-human
will rarely conceive
and even more rarely be able to raise
fempires.
On the rare occasion that they do,
the same general difficulties
faced by manpires
are faced by fempires.

SAFKINSOP.

"tonight's item to stoke" (aka TITS)
(pardon the French,
we've been a male dominated business
for centuries other than in Egypt and Syria
where powerful queens
like Cleopatra, Hatshepsut and Palmyra
inspired some of the great female vampire killers
modernly known as stokers.
All of this is to say
that we are changing
but acronyms die hard
especially, well, the ones that stick).
Returning to Safkinsop,

the evening TITS (couldn't resist)
this male vampire
had a file
as big as any bloodsucker in the city.

It goes without say that
his ECA (his estimated conversion amount)
was extremely high.

But that alone
is not what made him unique.
nor what made him a vampire of interest.

Safkinsop was our present vampire of interest
because he had developed a taste
for mortgage brokers
who were predatory lenders
during the Great Recession.
And the stokers
many of which
are inner city people of color
were disproportionately affected by that financial crises.

Therefore, given his selective 'throat type'
("STI"...that acronym
unlike TTS
is one we are pushing back against deleting
from the field manual)
Anyways, where was I
yes...throat type.
Stokers turned a blind eye
to Safkinsop
when he dined on mortgage lenders
jokingly saying
in closed company
that he was simply employing
his own method of reverse redlining.

With Dodd-Frank keeping mortgage lenders in line
and limiting the predatory nature of such lenders,
Safkinsop's pallet
shifted
from the political to the practical.
In place of mortgage lenders
he developed a taste for food delivery drivers
especially ones who delivered food on bikes.
The prevailing theory for this new
throat choice
was that it was Safkinsop's way
of developing an immunity to garlic
via indirect exposure.
I suppose he could smell it faintly
while the bikes were moving through
the city streets
and sustain the diluted whiffs of garlic
while he bit them in transit
always in transit.

You'd think that these attacks
would have garnered
attention sooner than they did.
Apparently New Yorkers getting
jumped on bikes
isn't too out of the ordinary.
People just carry on their business.
What changed things was demand.
Human delivery drivers in New York City
have great work ethic.
You give them a plastic bag
to wrap around their hands
and they will deliver food to your
doorstep in a blizzard.
Vampire delivery drivers
on the other hand
will not take any orders during the day.
And at night
they may take your order
but it is you who is on the menu.
All of this caused a citywide lunch crises.

The mayor got involved
gave some speeches
called on the police department
specifically "Police Aid"
aka the stokers.
Our unit was happy
to take on the assignment.
Stokers have an affinity
for helping anyone in the food business
since we see food as a main separator
between us and the bloodsuckers.
As a result,
Safkinsop became vampire enemy number 1.
That qualification mandates that
the stokers send in their big guns,
like me.

I'd like to say that when a stoker
is 'sent' somewhere
on orders to kill a vampire
that means we always
get to visit some obscure
castle atop snowcapped mountains
where we can take in nature
while getting our gothic architecture
fancy tickled
and writing off our travel as a tax deduction.
This isn't always true.

And it isn't for the lack of castles
in New York City.
Oddly enough
there are castles in New York City.
Uptown Manhattan's Cloisters, for instance,
has had vain vampires fighting over lodging
for their coffins
since Rockefeller
had the place constructed
in the 1930's.
Publically, vampires will claim
it's the influx of medieval art
that draws them to this sort of dwelling.
Privately, we think these Vampires
are doing their own version
of what Safkinsop is doing
when he bites delivery drivers carrying
garlic-heavy food.
In other words
these vampires in New York City castles
are working to develop a resistance
to their defects.

In this case
they are experimenting
with exposure
to the European stone
Cloisters is constructed of
which was shipped over
from Old World abbeys.
This seems to be their way
of getting indirectly acquainted
with Christianity
in eventual hope of warding off
their fears
of the crucifix.

But Safkinsop is too clever
to house himself
in such a popular location
where even a newly minted stoker
could potentially stoke him.
The only real similarity
between where he
put his head down to rest
in the daytime and Cloisters Castle
is the amount of stairs in both places.
The one's toward Safkinsop's lair though
do not lead to some majestic main hall.
They descend from the main floor
of a rundown Section 8 housing project
next to what is almost certainly
an intentionally broken elevator.

By the time me and Kimora, my apprentice,
reached the basement
boiler room
of that section 8
housing project
we were exhausted.
The reward greeting us
at the bottom
was blackness.
Nothing but blackness.
No surprise there.
But for Kimora adhering
to stoker protocol
since, with my sign-off,
she could be stoking as an apprentice
for the last time,
we wouldn't have bothered
to check the electric box.
It most certainly did not work
and was beyond repair.
If I didn't know
her ambitious nature
her over-precision would have annoyed me
would have come across as goody-goody.
Us stokers joke that
the more of a goody-goody you are
the sweeter your blood.
And the sweeter your blood
the more desirable dessert you are
for what you are stoking

Like I said, Kimora was a different story.
You see, Kimora had dreams of stoking
internationally.
To get a job doing that
she would need
to have stoked a recognizable vampire
like Safkinsop.

That is why I brought her along tonight
and didn't do the deed myself.
Along with a reputable stoking
Kimora also needed a recommendation
from a reputable stoker.
If she pulled this off tonight she would
kill both of those birds with one stoke.

Truth be told, on my recommendation alone
she could land any stoker job in America.
Stoker purists overseas though
would take more convincing.
They have historically turned their nose up
on American stoking.
This is because very few American vampires
have Before Christ (BC) 'undeathdays'
and therefore
very few American stokers
can boast of the prized 'BC stoke.'
To get that you would need to find
an indigenous stoker
that wasn't wiped out
alongside indigenous people
during the American saga
known broadly as human 'indian removal'.
Or you would need to travel
to the American extremes
deep into the Arctic
or deeper into the Amazon.

There are a few exceptions.
Kimora could try and find
an old world vampire
that emigrated from overseas.
The few that are left
reside in upper New England.
Small towns.
Feed mostly on southern skiers.
Big Red Sox fans.
In fact, the Green Monster was named
after an Old World Vampire
from Ireland
otherwise known as
'the Druid that decimated Southie'.
Kept residence in Boylston Street.
Stabbed himself in the heart
after Aaron bleepin' Boone
hit that homerun for the Yankees
in game 7 of the 2003 ALCS.
Silly Druid
would have kept going for another
few thousand years if he waited
one more year for the Sox.

You're probably thinking
that you're going to wait
another thousand years
for me to explain Vampire 'undeathdays'.

Apologies
allow me to explain:
A vampire's 'undeathday' is
the date the vampire
fully transforms
from a human into a vampire.
Depending on the toxicity
of the vampire's bite,
this transformation
can take days, weeks,
perhaps even months.

Amongst stokers
it is an unwritten rule
that you don't kill a vampire
anywhere near their 'undeathday.'
Sensitive as they are about their ages,
they grow restless
in their coffins leading up to it.

Sometimes the restlessness leading up to
'undeathday' is so bad
that Vampire insomnia sets in.

At that point
dealing with them
is about as safe
as throwing grease
on gas.

Along with taste,
this sensitivity to age
is another reason
why vampires prefer
to dine
on young people
with wet bites.

Kimora's prep for the night
required total assurance
that we were nowhere near
Safkinsop's 'undeathday'.
Other than in the most dire
of circumstances
a stoker will not pry open
the coffin of a vampire
within 6 months of its 'undeathday.'
Even with every precaution
the additional variables this could add
to completing a successful stoking
makes the job simply
too dangerous to attempt.

It's also simply too dangerous
to travel around in the dark
without functioning
electrical boxes.
That is, unless you fashion your own
alternative light source.

Kimora, tossing me my flashlight and headgear
and turning on Fang, our bomb disposal robot,
had rightly anticipated this.
Thanks to Fang rolling out of her backpack
our visibility returned.
We checked for scratched pipes
and teeth marks
and blood residue
around the basement boiler room.
Nothing.
No surprise there.
A smart vampire like Safkinsop
does their best to conceal
all evidence of their existence.
To stoke him
you need an expert, a master stoker,
able to detect the more subtle clues
that give away
the entrance to his secret passageway
and able
to track through
the subsequent
complex earthy burrow-maze
that leads to the coffin room.

To see what I saw
inspect what I inspected
is harder than it sounds.
And cannot be accomplished
without a lot of
on the job experience.
Remember
vampires are shapeshifters.

Therefore the secret passageway
entrance
could be a crack no bigger than what
a spider could crawl into
or fog particles could
blow underneath.
And that's only the beginning.
Once you find
the entrance itself
you have to figure out
a way through
without blowing the place to hell
and waking the vampire up,
because that entrance
is going to be strapped
with more explosives
than a fireworks barge
in the East River
on the Fourth of July.
So too for that matter
will be every step of the burrow
that isn't snared
or dressed with barbed wire
or other happy things
like pits full of spikes
the tips of which
are poisoned with
vampire venom.

Besides observing Kimora
for her performance evaluation and recommendation,
those were my responsibilities.
Kimora's responsibilities focused
more on what was to come later on
things like cracking the coffin
and stoking the vampire
all the while being mindful
of time
since every second was another second
closer to night
and we needed to render Safkinsop tonically immobile
before then.
More on that later.

As expected
the journey through the burrow
and into Safkinsop's coffin room
was like
laying siege to Kenilworth castle.
Thankfully, we arrived in ample time
for Kimora to get to work.
Also as expected,
space was tight.
Like most vampires
Safkinsop provided very little room
for any maneuvering around the coffin.
Kimora, well-trained in small spaces,
was hardly deterred.
Stoking isn't a job for the claustrophobic.
You have to be comfortable
in such closed conditions.
You also must be ready to wield a shovel
and be ready to dig.
Because on the occasion, like today,
when a bloodsucker
covered their own coffin in soil,
that's the only way to get to them.

This concerned me.
Despite being undead
vampires are rather hygienic.
Even though they don't shower
they don't stink
and even though they sleep
in the same clothes
that they wear every day
they are pretty put together
all things considered.
Plus they dislike dirt
more than one would think.
So if Safkinsop voluntarily
covered his coffin in soil
and would either have to mist through it
or dig up through it
for his evening escapades
it meant he was inconveniencing himself
for the sake of caution.
It meant he knew Stokers were coming. .

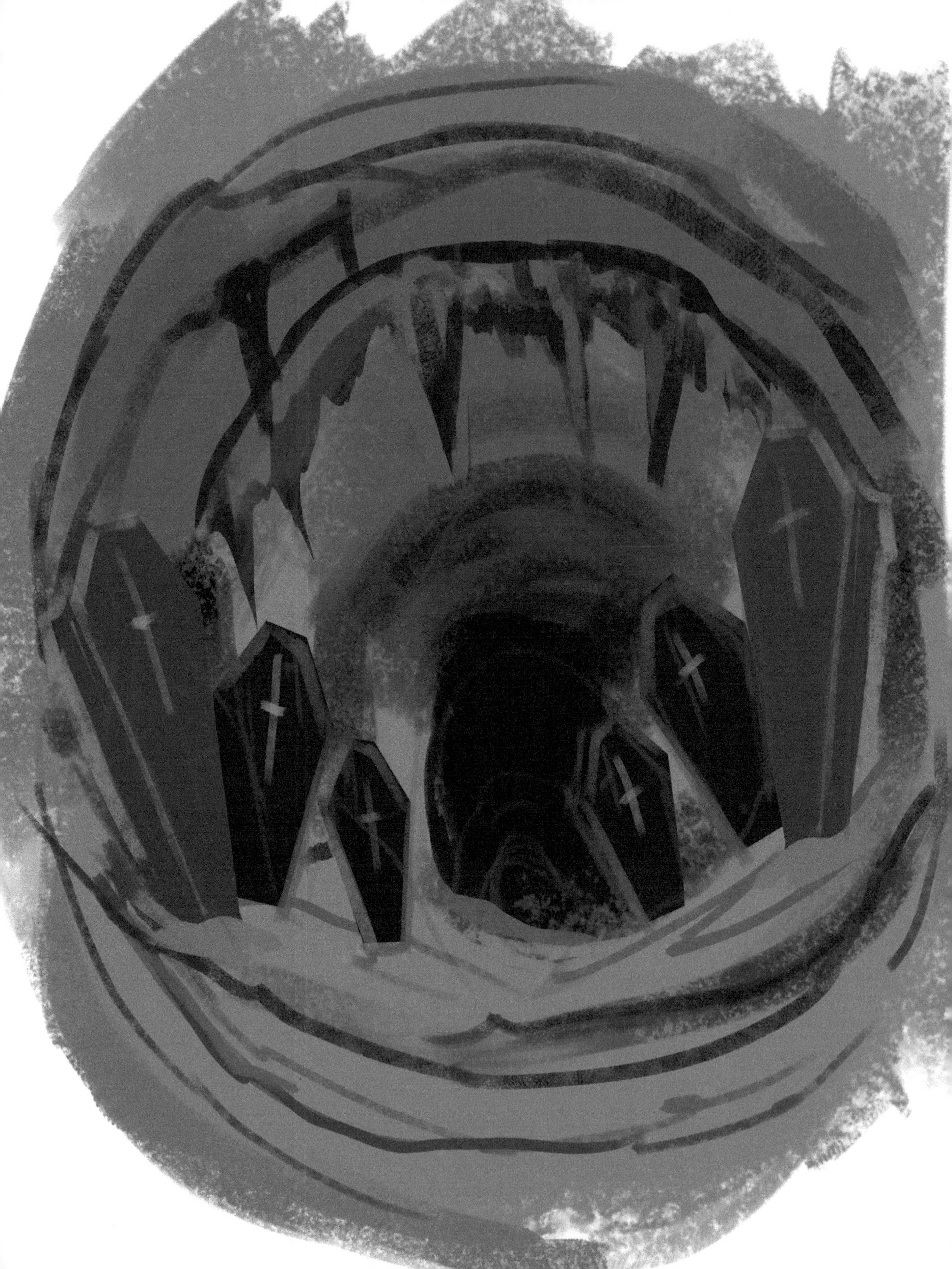

His buried coffin also concerned me
because digging soil
digs into time.
Hopefully it wasn't too far down
before we reached rock.
Vampires won't sleep on or beneath rock.
They need to sleep amongst their own grave soil.
Along with that, I worried we were
digging up the wrong coffin.
Vampires tend to bury
multiple decoy coffins
in different places along their burrow.
If you spend the day digging up
and then cracking the locks
of the wrong one,
you won't make it outside during daylight
which means you won't see daylight
again.

You also can't waste too much time
digging
when you need to be cracking locks.
Even for the master stoker,
those locks take time to crack.
Understand that neither
the real coffin nor the decoys
will be pinewood boxes
with padlocks.
No manpire on the black market
who constructs a killer vamp lock
will install it
on some old pinewood box.

Manpires
the most common purveyors
of vamp locks
like cash money.
In typical black-market fashion
they also love connecting
tying provisions to a purchase
meaning
if a vampire wants
the most updated expensive vamp lock
a vampire has to buy
the most expensive coffins
that come with it.

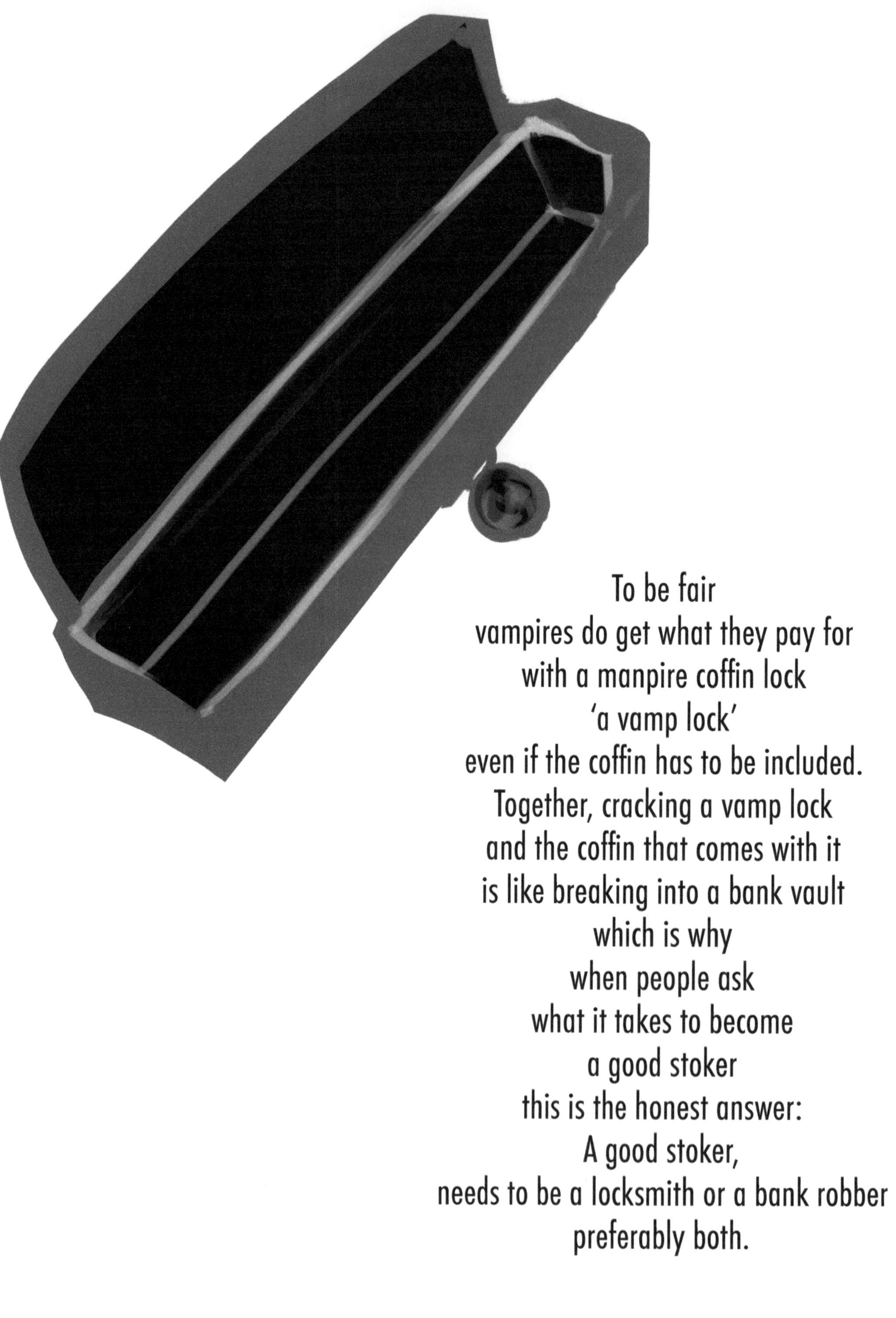

To be fair
vampires do get what they pay for
with a manpire coffin lock
'a vamp lock'
even if the coffin has to be included.
Together, cracking a vamp lock
and the coffin that comes with it
is like breaking into a bank vault
which is why
when people ask
what it takes to become
a good stoker
this is the honest answer:
A good stoker,
needs to be a locksmith or a bank robber
preferably both.

And on top of that
they need to know their way around
mobile applications.
Why mobile applications?
Remember earlier when I explained
that killing vampires
in most of the classical ways
is becoming harder and harder to do?
I am a renowned stoker.
Therefore, apprentices
'kill for'
my letter of recommendation
and when I say 'kill for'
I do not mean the required stoking
that Kimora was up to
in dealing with Safkinsop.

The weight of my recommendation
comes from my crowning achievement.
my discovery
of another way
a more efficient way
to kill vampires
using modern technology.

I'd like to say that the idea arose
out of some calling
some passion
to vanquish vampires.
The truth is less dramatic.
Like so many other great ideas
I sort of stumbled upon it accidentally.
If you haven't realized
I'm no idealist.
No freedom fighter.
Like a manpire
I too like my cash money,
always have.
In fact, it's why,
before I made my discovery
I spent quite a bit of time
hanging with manpires
and making "vamp locks" on the black market.
That's where the money was.
It's also where the vampires were.
So the job put me in touch with the clientele
on a regular basis.

One client, a female vampire,
long past child-rearing age,
became more than a client.
I fell in love with her,
have the dry bites
up and down my neck
to show for it.
My story is a common one.

You think young men like female humans
that are a little older,
cougars as they say?
Imagine how crazy they go for female vampires
that are far older
yet don't show their age.
We call them
sabertooths.
You look close enough upon a man's neck
and we all have a little damage to show
for our days
scoring with sabertooths
dabbling with death.
It might not get grandma's approval
but 'sabertoothing' isn't as culturally taboo
as paying for human sex workers.
The main reason is that
female vampires are all
sole proprietors.
So sabertooths don't need pimps.
And if you try anything on them
well
you won't be having dinner with them
you'll be dinner for them
While wet bites from
the more business-oriented sabertooths
are far less frequent than from
their male counterparts
sabertooths are more than capable
of delivering them.

As I said
I got myself involved with one of these
sabertooths.
and silly young me
I fell in love with her
this fempire
at the same time I was paying
for her services.

At the time
this didn't seem like
such a big deal.

Back then,
I had so much money from
working at the black market vamp shop-
a rare job for a human to have I may add-
that payment just seemed like a formality
the equivalent of what
any classy man would do
during the dating process
to pay for courtship.
My error was in not
seeing how unnatural
acting like this was for me.
I never have
and never will
be a classy man.
The second I started acting like one
is when I got into trouble.

Damn first loves.
They make you blind.
I found her, my fempire, so beautiful.
Yet when I said that
it got her all upset
because vampires cannot cast their own reflection
and see themselves.

There are a lot of theories for
why this is the case-
you can't reflect a soul you don't have;
mirrors used to be made of pure silver
and the purity of silver
prohibits the reflection
of something so impure-
to name a few.
I'm sure there are others.

To make her feel better
about this condition
this defect of non-reflection
I did the next best thing,
I started to paint her,
my beloved fempire.

I thought I was real smart
coming up with this idea
until I realized that the main reason
for all those famous painted portraits
both the ones lining museum walls
and the ones rotting
in the attics of aristocrats,
is that so many vampires
want to see themselves.
Fun fact
if you go to a portrait gallery
I'd say more than half of them
are vampire portraits.
Makes sense
that they'd be
the patrons
willing to spend the most money.
A fact of life is that sometimes
it is simply more money
that will produce more masterpieces.
It's also the only way to attract manpires
who were and are
the majority of portrait painters.
That's a dirty little secret of the art world
you won't hear from your college professors
until graduate school.

She told me this
and so many other secrets of the vampire
as she posed for me long into the night
in positions
most manpire portrait painters
could only dream about witnessing.
Granted those manpire portrait painters
also got paid to paint.
I did the opposite.
I paid her, my fempire,
my muse,
to pose.
Big difference.
The combination of
paying her to pose
along with her uncharacteristic free-spirit
as a vampire
(remember
they trend more towards enslaved spirits
than free-spirits)
allowed me to put every inch
of the vampire form
on canvas
in every position possible.

In doing so
I learned how to capture a vampire image
the way a camera would
the way
I became determined...
A CAMERA SHOULD!

This gave birth to my idea.
an idea I dedicated
the next few years of my life to,
an idea
that was as simple in theory
as it was difficult
to manufacture in practice.

But by the end
it was worth it
when I could finally say
that I had built
the first ever mobile phone adapter
and corresponding mobile app
capable of processing
a vampire's reflection.

When I believed the adapter/app
was finally ready
I thought nothing more appropriate
then for me and my love to
celebrate with our first

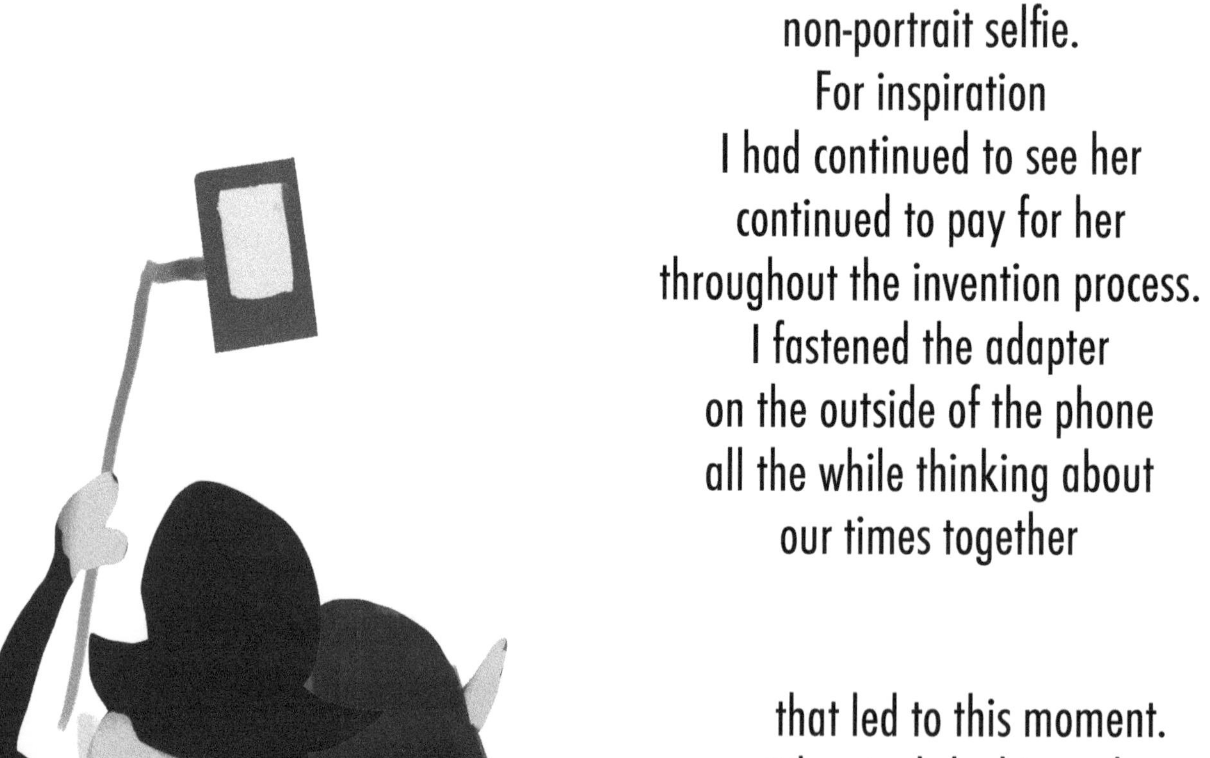

non-portrait selfie.
For inspiration
I had continued to see her
continued to pay for her
throughout the invention process.
I fastened the adapter
on the outside of the phone
all the while thinking about
our times together

that led to this moment.
When it clicked into place
the app automatically popped on screen.
It loaded.
I stretched out the selfie stick
and leaned both our faces in front
of the modified mobile phone camera.
Voila!

There we were,
my mug with a neck full of dry bites
and her beautiful face, figure
and mouth-closed smile
stretching from ear to ear,
her two pearly white
canines poking out her top lip,
the star of the shot.
With all of it finally available on screen
I expected bliss.

I did not get what I expected.
Rather than a jump for joy
stillness.
Rather than shouts of joy
silence.

At minimum
I hoped my contributions to the
undead
would grant me
a refund of sorts
for all the services
I paid her for
over the years.

She did none of this.
In fact
she did nothing at all.
Her face
her eyes
her mouth agape
were glued to the screen
trancelike
more lifeless than usual
completely catatonic.
Concerned

I hopped into bed and
asked that she follow.
She didn't move.
I'd like to say that ignoring me
was an abnormal response
to me summoning her to bed.
It was not.
What was unusual was the complete

lack of response
devoid of all protest.
She didn't move a muscle
until I went over to her
and fully guided her
back to 'our office'
as she liked (and I hated) to call it.

When even that received no response
I took the phone from her
and put it on the nightstand
moving it from her visual field.
She almost instantly returned
to normal consciousness.

This is when I realized
or shall I say discovered
something unknown to humankind
and perhaps to vampirekind
since either of our origins.

When a Vampire actually sees their reflection
they do what sharks do
when their snout is touched.
They enter into tonic immobility.
With her consciousness regained
from me pulling the phone from her
we did the deed
that I primarily paid her for.

By morning I woke up alone.
Nothing unusual about that.
Per our agreement
she always went home late at night
after I nodded off
so she could return to her coffin
before daylight.
What was different about this morning
was that while I was alone
she had never left.

She had just been reduced to
a pile of dust
on my duvet.

The morning sun
shining through my window,
got her.
And not for romantic reasons
not because she couldn't afford
to be away from me
for another morning.

The tell was that my phone
which I couldn't find at first
and doubled as my alarm
vibrated underneath the pile of dust
at its regularly scheduled time.
Clearly her cause of death
was vanity.
The little narcissa
had grabbed my mobile phone
off the nightstand after
I fell asleep
installed the adapter
turned on the app
and watched herself
on screen until morning
when the sun
that pure
perfect killer
of all things Vampire
came up
and caused her demise.

Looking back
I think that was the best thing
for both of us.
Well, I won't speak for her.

After I fed her to my dustbuster
that didn't seem right.
But I will speak for myself.

The second I saw
her powdery remains
slide to and from
the different wrinkles on my duvet
I knew I wasn't looking at dust
I was looking at pure cash money.

22 months later both my app and my adapter
had patent numbers.
During the approval process
I received job offers
from every federal and state stoker program
in the nation.
Infinite solicitations from foreign counterparts
came shortly thereafter.

The only country that didn't
offer me a gig
was Vatican City.
To ensure there were no hard feelings
on that decision,
His Holiness called me and explained
that because the Vatican had so many preventative measures
already in place
to defend against bloodsuckers,
good conscience instructed him
to allow my expertise
elsewhere
somewhere less prepared.
With that holy water under the bridge
the Pope used the rest of our conversation
to offer a few
suggestions on stoking based on his
own experiences.

If there were any doubts before
his Holiness made one thing very clear:
vampire resistance
to silver bullets and wooden stakes
had clearly gone global.
Desperation had set in.
Yours truly put an end to that.

Nearly overnight
my app revolutionized
the stoking business
Sure, stokers still holstered
silver bullet guns
and hung
stakes and hammers
around their utility belts.
But they did it more
for style and tradition
the way a marine wears a sword
than out of present utility.

Beyond the getups
and the pageantry
day-to-day stoker training
shifted from
carpentry for stake-building
and marksmanship for shooting silver bullets
to big tech
and to computer hacking
especially with respect to
cracking 'vamp locks' and
utilizing robotics for
burrow bomb disposal.

This shift in skillset
brought with it
a shift in the sort of person
attracted to the stoker business.
Geeks,
barely able to get through
the physical parts of the academy
began to dominate the field.

The old field
far more macho in nature
was one that
neither myself
nor Kimora for that matter
could play on.

If things stayed as they were
she'd probably be at Google.
I'd probably be back on the black market
making vamp locks
or working a high-end coffin room
and to be honest
nobody would even be attempting
to stoke Safkinsop.

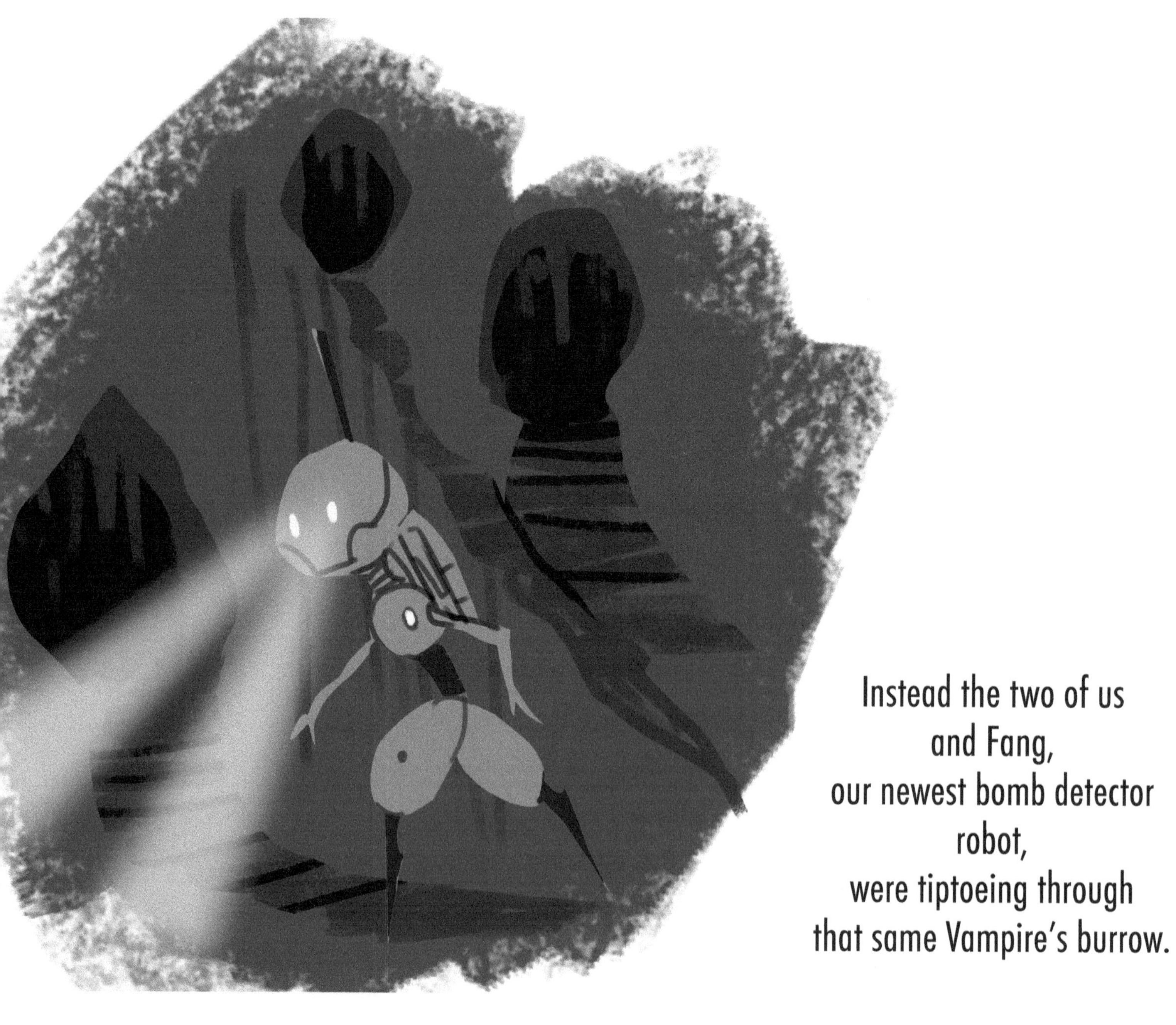

Instead the two of us
and Fang,
our newest bomb detector
robot,
were tiptoeing through
that same Vampire's burrow.

A burrow full of
false passageways
and
bombs
and camouflaged pits
and snares
that could trigger
anything from
spears
to the firing of automatic weapons
to the emission of deadly chemicals.
And we were doing all this tiptoeing
while at the same time
carefully documenting
each safe step we took
in order to duplicate it on the way back
from the coffin room
when joined by
an additional
tonically immobile
yet inherently hostile
member of our party.

By the time we reached our destination
Kimora passed all the disarmament
and detection
requirements
on the stoker exam.
I didn't need to tell her this fact.
At this juncture,
by simply being alive
she already knew.

I imagine that is why a smile
came over her face
when we entered the coffin room.
I mean, why else would it?

Resist what comes to mind
when you envision such a place.
Safkinsop did not have organs playing.
There weren't dimly lit torches
encased equally around the walls
waiting for an oil change.
The vampire was less concerned
with aesthetic
more concerned with limiting stoker maneuverability inside.
Kimora, necessarily hunched over
in the narrow lair
spread her tools out on the fresh soil.
Meanwhile I took the liberty
to plug her computer into a splitter.
One side of the splitter ran to

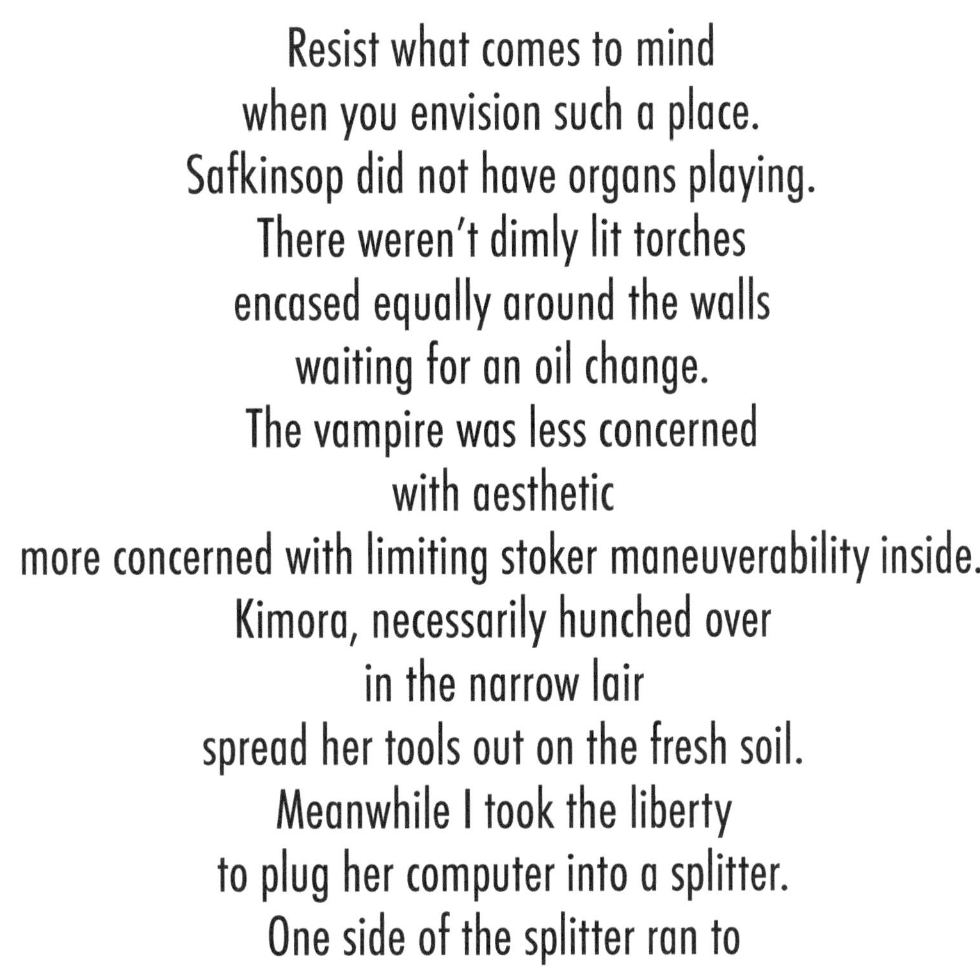

the coffin's 'vamp-lock'
The other side of the splitter
ran to Fang (remember Fang?)
for diagnostics.

Kimora got to coding
or shall we say hacking
the 'vamp-lock'
as soon as the little robot spit out enough particulars.
The work was performed
in silence
to adhere to industry best practices.
Every click of the keyboard
kept below a certain decibel.
Every metal tool coated in rubber
to reduce clang.

Because even though it's true
that Vampires are deep sleepers
they are undead sleepers
not dead sleepers.
If you make enough noise
you'll be greeted with
beady red eyes
rather than closed lids
which means game over.

For proof of this fact
look no further than
modern vampire coffin design.
The most basic black market models
come equipped with alarm systems
that blare loud enough
to alert a distant boat in a storm
let alone a sleeping vampire.
Once a stoker removes the coffin hinges
they have to deprogram such alarm systems
pronto.
Because in seconds it will start clanging
and when it clangs
that vampire is rising out of
its coffin like a pissed off cobra
responding to a musically disinclined
snake charmer.

A few logic bombs
malware installations
credential recycling and dictionary attacks later
allowed Kimora and I to slip off the coffin hinges.
No beady red eyes greeted us when we did
which meant we were quiet enough
to continue working.
Safkinsop lay inside
sleeping like a dead baby.

At this point
suppressing instinct
remembering your training
managing impulse control
is everything.

It's natural to want to go Rambo
on the bloodsucker
and stab it,
and shoot it,
and burn it,
blow it up.

The modern stoker
must have the discipline
to conform to banal modernity
and leave their medieval toys behind.
They must unholster their mobile phone
open the right mobile application
install the right adapter
and start their crypt walk.
The Crypt Walk is what we call
the journey a stoker takes
alongside a vampire they've rendered
tonically immobile.
The walk starts in darkness and ends
in daylight
at a solar barbeque.

Thankfully Kimora trusted the practice.
She did not listen to her inner Rambo.
For reasons previously discussed
she knew that
wooden stakes
and silver bullets were a bad idea.

Below is a brief primer on why
other more practical methods
traditionally employed
to kill vampires are also flawed
and why a crypt walk
to a solar barbeque
is the best way to stoke in the 21st century.

Consider the problems with beheading.
You open the casket
assemble your little handy dandy
miniature guillotine
you scream
"off with your heads"
Queen of Hearts
Robespierre
Marie Antoinette style.
Except the guillotine that you somehow
managed to drag through the no-man's land
that is a Vampire burrow
full of landmines
doesn't slide through a vampire neck
like it does a human neck.
A vampire neck is much harder.
To get through one
you'll need a diamond cutter saw
one of those bad boys
that you've seen (and certainly heard)
cutting patio bricks on a masonry job site.
You'll also need some time
time you don't have before the vampire wakes
to finish the job.

A laser would be quicker.
But they are so cost prohibitive
and so heavy and bulky
that it's probably easier rolling a guillotine
through the burrow to the intended destination.
Plus budget-wise it's a lot easier
to get every stoker a mobile phone
than every stoker a thousand-pound laser.

In any case
let's assume a successful beheading.
Don't celebrate too soon.
That alone won't kill it.
To kill it
you have to grab that head
and that body
and lug all that undead weight
back upstairs
into the daylight.

PRECAUTIONS

even if you take all the precautions
meaning you stuff a vampire's mouth full of garlic
poke its eyes through
with a pair of crucifixes
and secure it in a suitcase
these are temporary stunning measures
none of which
the vampire's body
nearby
and angry
and still equipped with speed and supernatural strength
will be happy about.

Chances are
the body will begin to
wreak havoc in the burrow
like a derailing freight train
sliding through a tunnel.

Not to mention
crucifixes and garlic
are temporary remedies,
stunners rather than killers,
meaning the Vampire's head
will at some point
regain composure
inside the suitcase
long enough to summon the body
to release it
to fuse it back together.

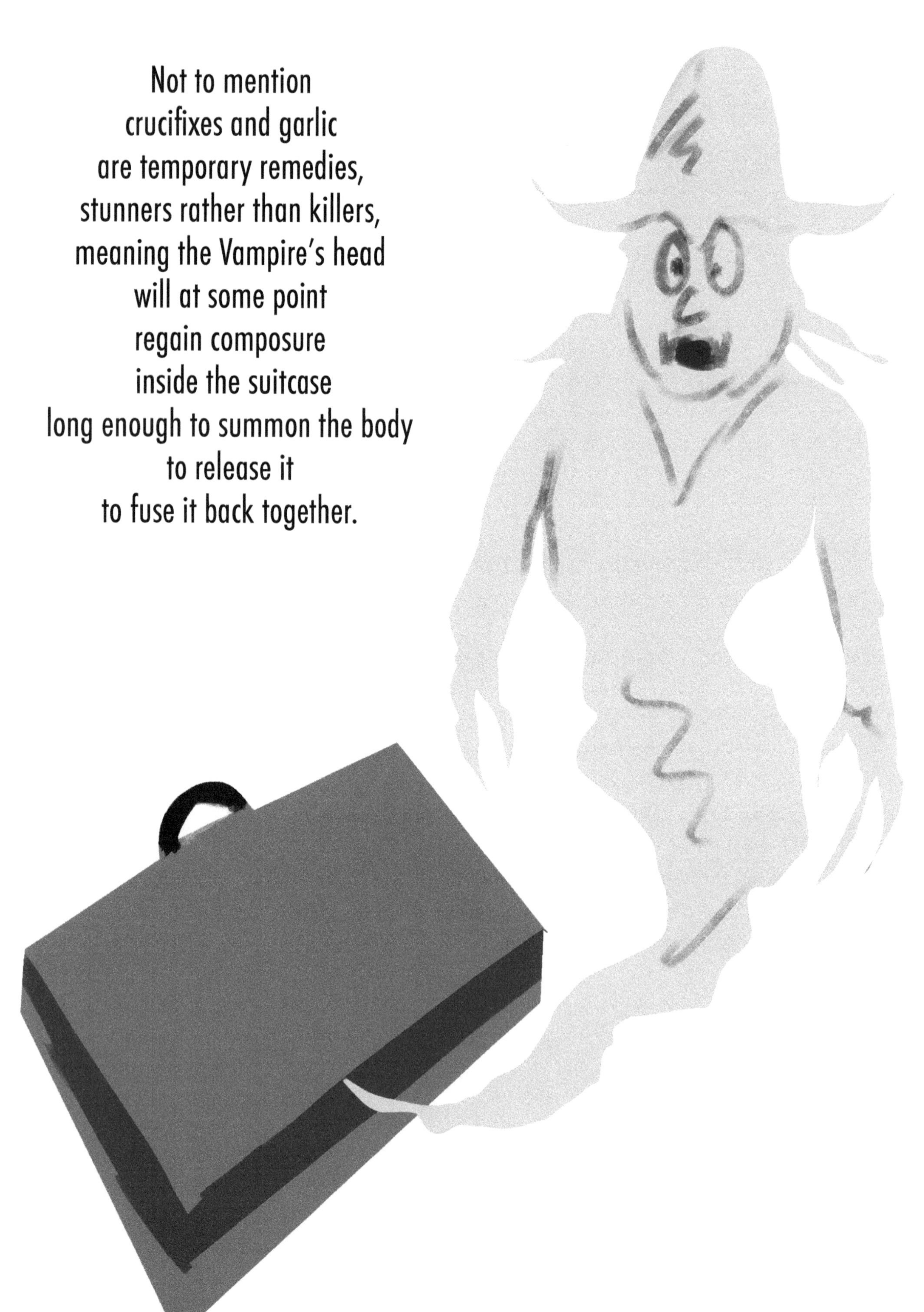

More disciplined vampires like Safkinsop
may bypass this sequence of events altogether
and simply turn to mist
and seep out the suitcase
like steam escaping a tea kettle.
The dangers of such mist are many,
none more terrifying than creating
an unnavigable burrow
that cannot be pierced by manmade light.

Unable to see,
stokers will wander
off in the wrong direction
until falling into a pit
or a snare
or on top of a bomb.
Although the explosion may make both you and the vampire splatter,
it is your splatter that is permanent.
The vampire's splatter is already regenerating by the time it hits the wall.
In moments they'll be
good as new.

With all that considered, why not just burn em', you say?
Unfortunately, the same principles apply to
burning as beheading.
A vampire will shapeshift once it goes on fire.
In the event that it decides to burn into dust
it will shapeshift after burning into dust
and do so long before the crypt walk
hits the homestretch.
Day 1 of stoker training teaches you
that the effects of the Sun on a vampire
are not the same as the effect of fire on a vampire.
This is because it is not the heat
but the natural light from the sun
daylight
that kills a vampire.
Moonlight or lightning
both generally creatures of night
do not have that effect
nor does human-made light for that matter.

When you take all the variables
into consideration
that come with trying to kill a vampire
it becomes clear that
your best chance
at a successful stoking
is to get the vampire to crypt walk.
Kimora demonstrated proper practices
for initiating this process to perfection.
She unplugged fang (Remember Fang?)
along with all other cords
attached to the coffin.
Then she grabbed her phone
from her pocket
installed the adapter onto the camera lens
and opened the corresponding app.

IT WAS TIME
TO WAKE SAFKINSOP UP.

Even though they're deep sleepers
if you're intentional about waking the
vampire
after the coffin is open
it's easy enough to do.
However, doing so impulsively
can be a lethal mistake.
As gratifying as it may feel
to slap them
or punch them,
doing so will startle them,
making it harder
to get the camera app on your phone
directly in front of the vampire's face
and initiate tonic immobility.

Rather than physical stimuli
making noise
is the ideal method to wake a vampire.
Not noise like the coffin alarm either.
That noise is designed to startle them
to bring the Vampire
to immediate attention
so that they can defend themselves from a stoker
during a coffin break.

It's much smarter to wake vampires
with something they find soothing.
Creating this type of controlled environment
makes for easier inducement into tonic immobility.
A stoker finds out what a vampire finds soothing
and what they want to wake up to
after they disarm the coffin alarm system
and hack into the coffin's internal hard drive.
Surprisingly, death metal is not always queued up.
During my time stoking
I've heard every type of wake-up noise—
music, audiobooks, anything.
Safkinsop, for instance, had an affinity for NPR.

Kimora flipped on Fang (remember Fang?)
to stream
newest episode of "All things Considered."
Safkinsop stirred when the familiar intro music played.
By the time the hosts provided opening statements
Kimora had her mobile phone
right in front of the vampire's face.
Safkinsop's beady red eyes glazed over
in that manner typical of tonic immobility.
So began the most dangerous phase of modern stoking.
THE CRYPT WALK.

There's no easy way to say it.
The crypt walk is brutal.
It starts when the stoker
first wakes the vampire in their burrow
at last light of the day
and continues all night
ending only when the stoker
gets the vampire outside
into the daylight
beginning the solar barbeque.

For less dangerous vampires
without adequate lair defenses
the actual physical crypt walk is fast.
It's waiting for the sunlight afterward,
that's what takes up most of the time
that's what presents most of the danger.

Absent certain exceptions
those stokings are carried out by junior stokers starting out.
This is because the task
which is essentially keeping the phone
in front of the vampire's face
and waiting until sunrise
does not demand the skill of a master stoker.
The main dangers here
dozing off
sneezing
having bathroom break complications
are manageable for rookies.

That is not to say that mishaps
while seemingly minor
cannot be tragic.
Even the slightest disturbance runs the risk
of moving the phone
from in front of the vampire's face,
thus undoing tonic immobility,
thus doing a stoker in.

Alternatively, when dealing with a very dangerous vampire
like Safkinsop
equipped with burrow defenses reminiscent of Fort Knox
the crypt walk will take all night
maybe more
maybe two nights
so a stoker must be conscious of time
not because tonic immobility runs out
indeed absent stoker error
a vampire in tonic immobility will stay in tonic immobility
but because more time spent stoking means more time
for stoker error.

Along with watching her step
and Safkinsop's step
to avoid

trips and falls that could lead to
explosions, poison pits,
snares and other traps,

Kimora was watching
for the newest
and yes more dangerous
vampire defenses:

I speak of counter cyber-attacks.

Counter cyber-attacks designed
to corrupt the camera app
or the camera lens
or the adapter hookup
long enough
to allow a vampire
to exit its state of tonic immobility.
Thanks to Fang (remember Fang?)
we had a pretty good handle on
defending against off-the-shelf proprietary options
that came as part of the standard 'vamp-lock' warranty.
The bigger danger was encountering
viruses of a more unique nature.
Most of the time these came from manpires
active on the dark web.

Despite all the training,
and all the precautions,
a stoker could always be compromised
by such counter cyber-attacks.

In fact, if a stoker was going to be Legosi-ed
meaning killed in action
being 'cybered' was how we all wanted to go.
Other alternatives
such as getting wrapped around a landmine
came with certain stigmas.
When that happened to an experienced stoker
it generally sounded like laziness.
Laziness though was more excusable than negligence.
Usually this came in the form of
poor preparation.

Not ensuring proper screen brightness
so that the Vampire could actually see their reflection?
NEGLIGENCE.

Not checking for potential automatic
hardware or software updates
on your mobile phone
that could cause random restarts?
NEGLIGENCE.

Improper mobile phone ventilation
causing phone to heat up and drop from your hand?
NEGLIGENCE.

Substance abuse causing shaky hands
that throw off tonic immobility?
NEGLIGENCE.

Not disabling push notification pop-ups?
NEGLIGENCE.

Not disabling text message pop-ups from lovers
or winy ex-lovers?
NEGLIGENCE.

Failure to monitor time
so that when you throw a vampire outside
you aren't doing so when it's still dark?
NEGLIGENCE.

ALL PREVENTABLE ACTS.
All have led to innumerable Legosis.

I watched Kimora avoid all these mishaps
with pride.
She walked Safkinsop past the passageway entry
and into the boiler room
and up the Section 8 housing steps
and finally
past the doors
and outside.

However, while Kimora accounted for time
she did not account for
weather
or more precisely
the day's astrological events.

As a result, Kimora walked Safkinsop
outside
at the exact same time
a total solar eclipse
blocked out the sun
making everything black
and keeping Safkinsop
alive
long enough
to lunge at Kimora's neck.

Thankfully
stokers are prohibited
from being child-rearing age.
And so
when Safkinsop
went for the throat of Kimora
he delivered a multi-minute
lustful bite
dry bite
last bite
before the sun poked back
over the moon
and started to shine.
Solar barbeque.

THE END

READ MORE BOOKS
BY DAVID O'BOYLE

available at davidoboyles.com

NOVELS

Mooncalfs

SHORT STORY COLLECTIONS

Transient Visitors: Month 1 of 12,
a Collection of Very Tiny Tales, Short Story Collection 2021

Transient Visitors: Month 2 of 12,
a Collection of Very Tiny Tales, Short Story Collection 2024

CHILDREN'S BOOKS

Friends from Other Flowerpots

Finboy

The Leprechaun who Wore Other Hats

Cricket's Quartet

In Defense of Sock Monsters

Pluto's Plea for Planethood

Giants of the South Pole

Friends from Other Flowerpots Part II: the Interrogation of the Wasp